WHAT HAPPENED HERE?

TUDOR FARMHOUSE

Elizabeth N

Photographs by Maggie Murray
Illustrations by Gillian Clements

Contents

A & C BLACK · LONDON

Who lived here?

In Tudor times, about 500 years ago, most people lived in small villages and worked in the countryside. Almost everybody was a farmer. Many rich farmers paid other people to farm their land. Some farmers, called yeoman farmers, owned small farms. They worked the land themselves with the help of their families, farmworkers and servants. Even the poorest people kept a few animals and grew crops in their gardens.

Life was very hard. Things we take for granted such as lavatories, running water and proper drains were almost unknown. Most houses had no glass in the windows. Many people did not have enough healthy food to eat. If the summer was wet, the harvest was bad. There was not enough food the following winter and thousands of people starved.

The children in this book wanted to know what it was like to live in a Tudor farmhouse. They began their investigation at the Weald and Downland Open Air Museum in West Sussex. Here they visited two real Tudor farmhouses which have been rebuilt at the museum. You can read the story of how these farmhouses were moved to the museum in the time-line on pages 6 and 7.

The barn was used for storing crops. When it was empty it may have been used for sheltering animals.

The windows of the farmhouse did not have any glass in them.

The orchard with apple and pear trees.

This shows what a farmhouse might have looked like in Tudor times. The picture is based on two houses at the Weald and Downland Open Air Museum. Both houses were built by yeoman farmers over 500 years ago.

The outside including the walls, windows and roof belong to a house called Bayleaf. It is similar to many farmhouses built just before the Tudor period. The inside including the chimney, hearth and the pantry belong to a farmhouse called Pendean. It is typical of the end of the Tudor period.

Carts and wagons were kept here.

farmyard

well

The farmer, his wife and children slept upstairs.

the pantry

Bees were kept in beehives.

Farmworkers slept by the fire.

the bake oven

the chimney with the hearth below

This room might have been the hall or parlour.

The walls of this farmhouse are made of wattle and daub. Wattle is thin hazel stems woven in and out like a basket. The wattle was plastered with daub, a mixture of earth, lime, cow dung, chopped straw and water.

vegetables, fruit, herbs

How do we know about the Tudor farmhouse?

The people who work at the museum have pieced together many different types of evidence so they can show visitors what life was like 500 years ago. They have filled the houses with exact copies of Tudor furniture and other objects. They even farm areas of the land near the farmhouses using some of the methods and farming tools the Tudors used.

Books, paintings and drawings

Many books have survived from the Tudor period. Diaries written at the time are especially useful because they tell us what people did. Recipe books tell us what people ate and how food was cooked. Books about farming describe how animals were reared, which crops were grown, and how farming tools were used. Paintings and drawings show us a lot about how people lived in Tudor times and what they wore.

Most farm animals have changed a great deal since the Tudor period. But this Old English goat is thought to be very similar to goats in Tudor times.

Lists of possessions

When somebody died, family, friends and neighbours made lists of the dead person's possessions. They wrote down and valued everything they saw. These lists, called probate inventories, tell us a lot about what Tudor people owned and what they thought was important.

This probate inventory lists the ▶ possessions of a man who lived in another Tudor house which is now in the Weald and Downland Open Air Museum. The list includes bacon, and half a hundredweight (about 25.5 kilos) of salted butter.

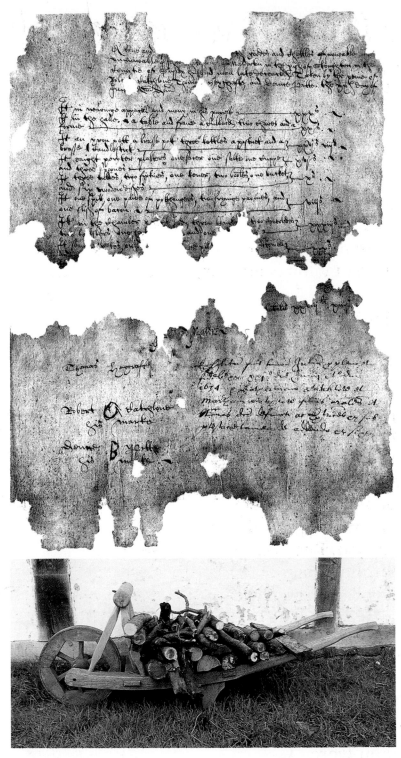

Objects

There are many thousands of objects, including furniture, weapons, coins and clothes which have survived from the Tudor period. Many of them can be seen in museums all over the country.

Archaeology gives us lots of clues about the past. The remains of a Tudor wheelbarrow were found in an archaeological dig in London. Workers at the museum used them to build an exact copy.

Time-lines

The first time-line shows some of the important events which took place during Tudor times. The second time-line shows some of the important events in the history of Bayleaf and Pendean, up to the present day.

Main events, ideas and inventions

1477

1477 William Caxton sets up the first printing press in England. Books no longer have to be written out by hand and they become cheaper. More people able to own books.

1485–1509 HENRY VII is the first Tudor king.

Shipbuilding is an important industry right through the Tudor period.

1509–1547 HENRY VIII is king.

Art and architecture become important. Members of the royal family and merchants built magnificent palaces and houses. Artists invited from Europe to paint portraits and decorate royal palaces.

Chimneys become very popular. Bricks, which have not been used as a building material since Roman times, are now made in large numbers. This means brick chimneys which keep rooms smoke free can be built into timber-framed houses.

1534 Parliament declares Henry VIII Head of the Church of England. Roman Catholic monasteries are closed. New Church of England services are started.

1545 The warship *Mary Rose* sinks on her way to fight the French. Over 400 men are drowned.

1547–1553 EDWARD VI is king.

Church services now said in English instead of Latin.

English prayer book used for the first time.

New grammar schools set up to teach boys from rich families to read and write.

Events at Bayleaf and Pendean

1405

1405–1430 Sometime during this period Bayleaf is built. It becomes the home of Henry Bailly. It looks very much as it does in the museum. The main room is a large hall which is heated by an open fire set in the middle of the floor. There is an opening in the roof to let the smoke out.

1575-1600 Around this time there is a lot of building at Bayleaf. The roof timbers are taken out so that a new chimney can be put in. Upstairs rooms are added at the same time.

Pendean built around this time. It is a very ordinary house, so no records survive telling us who lives there.

About **1800** Pendean is made into two cottages. Later it is made into a single farmhouse again.

1967 Bayleaf is in danger of being destroyed. It stands in an area which is to be flooded by a new reservoir.

6

1549 Poor people in eastern England rebel. They are protesting about high rents and low wages for farmworkers.

1553–1558 MARY I is queen.

Mary tries to re-introduce the Roman Catholic Church. Church services said in Latin.

About **1555**. Steel sewing needles replace needles made of wire. This makes embroidery easier and allows more delicate work to be done.

1558–1603 ELIZABETH I is queen.

Elizabeth becomes 'Governor' of the Church of England. Church services said in English again.

1564–1616 William Shakespeare writes at least 38 plays and many short poems called sonnets. Many of his plays are performed in the Globe Theatre which opened in London in 1599.

1577–80 Sir Francis Drake becomes one of the first people to sail right round the world.

1578–1657 William Harvey, one of the first doctors to dissect dead bodies, discovers how the heart pumps blood round the human body.

1588 A great fleet of ships, called the Spanish Armada, is sent by King Philip II of Spain to invade England. The English Navy defeats the Armada.

1601 The most important Poor Law is passed. Each parish has to look after its own poor. People in each parish have to pay money to help.

Bayleaf is given to the Weald and Downland Open Air Museum.

Bayleaf is carefully taken down and re-built at the museum exactly as it had been first built.

1973 Pendean is in danger of being destroyed. It stands in an area which is being dug for sand.

Pendean is taken down carefully. All the timbers and bricks are numbered so that the house can be fitted together again just like a giant jigsaw.

Pendean is rebuilt exactly as it had been first built.

How the farmhouse was built

Tudor houses were made of materials which the builders could easily find close by. The farmhouses at the museum were built by putting up a framework of oak timbers and filling in the spaces with other materials. Houses built in this way are called timber-framed houses.

Timber frames were often made of oak because in Tudor times oak trees grew in many parts of England. Oak is very strong and doesn't rot easily.

The Tudor builders made their timber-framed houses in sections. First they cut down the trees and trimmed off the branches. Then they sawed the trunks into lengths, and took them to where the house was being built. Here they shaped the timbers, cut the joints, and bored holes to take the oak pegs which held the joints secure. They marked all the timbers so that they knew where each piece fitted.

The children discovered that Tudor builders marked out and cut the joints very carefully so the timbers in the frame fitted tightly together. Tudor builders used different joints for different parts of a building.

The builders hauled the timbers upright into position using ropes and pulleys. By examining the walls in the farmhouses, the children saw that the Tudor builders had filled the spaces between the timbers with materials such as brick or wattle and daub.

Tudor builders used ropes and pulleys to hoist the timber frames into position, just as these museum workers are doing.

Both farmhouses at the museum have roofs made of clay tiles. This boy discovered that the tiles overlapped one another to keep out the rain. Wooden pegs stopped the tiles sliding off the roof.

9

Working the farm

In Tudor times the roads were very bad. A journey to and from the nearest town could take several days. Most people stayed in the country and went into the nearest town only a few times a year. There were no shops nearby so everything the farmer, his family and workers wanted had to be grown, reared or made on the farm.

Many Tudor farmers grew grain such as wheat, barley and rye. Most farmers kept animals. The children saw animals similar to those raised by Tudor farmers. They learned that the Tudor animals were much smaller and scrawnier than animals they would see on a modern farm.

Tudor farmers kept goats, cows and sheep for milk and meat. They kept hens for meat and eggs. They used horses for carrying, for riding, and for pulling loads. Animals also provided leather, horn to make beakers, and bone which was made into useful objects such as combs.

The children fed pigs kept in a pen near Bayleaf. The pig keeper told them that even the poorest Tudor farmers kept pigs to kill for meat, and that pork sausages were very popular in Tudor times. The pigs were not kept in pens. They were driven into the woods to find food, such as acorns and roots, for themselves.

Tudor farmers kept goats for meat and milk. The children noticed that the Tudor-style fence was strongly made to keep the animals in. The fence was made of planks set close together and pegged into position on rails. Other Tudor-style fences nearby were made of wattle like the walls of Bayleaf, but without the daub.

Farmers kept cattle for heavy work, such as pulling ploughs. Cattle were so useful that they were not killed for meat until they were too old to work.

The animals were kept in back yards or farmyards. People could also graze their animals on common ground which belonged to everyone. Most Tudor farmhouses had large gardens where the farmers grew their own fruit, vegetables and herbs.

Growing food

In Tudor times most houses had gardens. Tudor gardens were used for growing food, not for relaxing in.

The garden at Bayleaf, which was looked after by the farmer's wife, was big enough to grow vegetables to last the household through the winter.

The vegetable plots were laid out with narrow paths in between so that the farmer's wife could reach across without damaging the growing vegetables.

These children pulled up a leek for a Tudor vegetable stew called pottage. Most people in Tudor times, whether they were rich or poor, ate pottage every day. Pottage also contained garlic, parsley, cabbage, onions and other fresh vegetables. Sometimes the cook added meat.

The Tudors fertilised the ground with farmyard and human manure. The contents of a Tudor lavatory were not flushed away. They fell into a dung pit under the lavatory seat. The children shovelled muck out of the pit and spread it on the earth. It was hard work. If the muck had been real human dung, it would have been very smelly, too!

We know from Tudor books and pictures that what Tudor people did each day depended on the season. Men did most of the heavy work in the fields but women did most of the gardening.

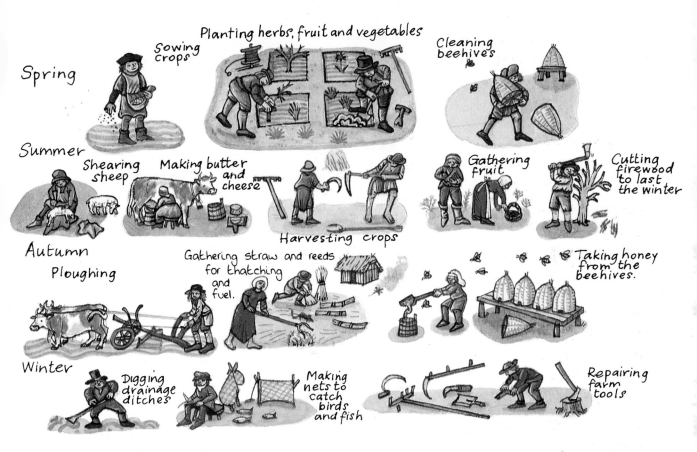

Spring — Sowing crops — Planting herbs, fruit and vegetables — Cleaning beehives

Summer — Shearing sheep — Making butter and cheese — Harvesting crops — Gathering fruit — Cutting firewood to last the winter

Autumn — Ploughing — Gathering straw and reeds for thatching and fuel. — Taking honey from the beehives.

Winter — Digging drainage ditches — Making nets to catch birds and fish — Repairing farm tools

The farmer's wife dealt with most of the illnesses and injuries amongst her own family and servants. She used herbs from the garden to make medicines and ointments. She used other herbs to preserve food, to flavour stews and salads, and to make herbal teas. She also threw herbs over the floors of the farmhouse, on top of the rushes, and sprinkled them in cupboards to make rooms smell sweet.

Most Tudors kept beehives in a quiet part of the garden so that animals and people did not disturb the bees. The honey was used to sweeten food, while the beeswax was used to make candles and polish. It was also used in cures and as a means of making things watertight.

Going to the mill

The miller showed the children a piece of machinery called a hopper. Grain is poured into the hopper and falls between the turning millstones. The millstones ground the grain into flour. Tudor millers were not paid with money. Instead they took a share of the grain they milled.

In Tudor times the staple, or main, food people ate was bread. People living in the country could not go to a shop to buy loaves. They had to make their own. After they had harvested the wheat they beat, or threshed, it to separate the grain from the stalks. Before they could eat the grain, it had to be ground into flour. This meant a trip to the mill.

Once the grain had been milled into flour, it was taken home to be baked into bread. Wheat flour made the best bread. But wheat only grows on the best soil, so wheat flour was very expensive. Most people ate bread, called maslin, which was made from a mixture of wheat and stronger-tasting rye flour. The poor ate bread made from ground peas or beans. In times of famine, people ate bread made from ground acorns.

▲ The children found that freshly milled flour felt much coarser than the fine, white flour we buy in packets from supermarkets. They were surprised to learn that a Tudor baker sifted the flour through a coarse cloth to remove the bran. Today bran is thought to be the healthiest part of bread, and our bakers put it back in.

Many people did their own baking. The cook kneaded the flour with salt, yeast and water in a trough to make it into dough. The dough was shaped into loaves, pricked, and left to rise for a while. The bread was baked in the bake-oven which was usually built into the fireplace of most houses.

◀ The children found a bake-oven in Pendean, built into the fireplace. The Tudors used ovens like this one to bake bread and pastries. The cook lit a brushwood fire inside the oven. When the oven reached a high enough temperature, the cook raked out the ashes. The bread was put in to bake while the oven was still very hot.

Storing food

Today we can store food for months, even years. We use refrigeration, freezing, drying, bottling and canning to stop food going bad. In Tudor times these ways of storing food had not been invented. The Tudors ate well in summer and autumn when there was plenty of food growing. But they had much less to eat during the winter and in early spring.

The children investigated the pantry in Bayleaf. They realised that this was one of the coolest rooms in the house and so would be a good place to store food. Pots, cooking equipment and barrels of ale were also stored here.

The Tudors salted meat or smoked it over the fire in much the same way that we preserve bacon, ham and some kinds of fish today. They also salted butter and stored it in barrels. We know that many Tudor people thought preserved food was valuable because they left butter, cheese and bacon to friends and relatives in their wills.

These children tried storing some food in the Tudor way. They strung onions together to be hung up. The onions were cut off as they were needed. The children also picked large bunches of herbs and hung them up to dry.

This girl plucked a pigeon. She found that the small feathers were quite difficult to pull out. In Tudor times, pigeons were kept in dovecots and provided meat in the winter.

The Tudors could not grow and store enough animal food, or fodder, to feed all their animals through the winter. In the autumn they kept alive only the best animals which gave milk, pulled loads, or were used for breeding. They killed the rest of their cattle, sheep and goats. They salted or smoked the meat to eat in the winter. Pigs, which were able to find food for themselves whatever the season, were kept all year round to be killed whenever people needed meat.

Preparing and cooking food

In Tudor times some large farmhouses had a room which was used as a kitchen. In other houses preparing and cooking food was done in the main room. Water for washing and cooking food had to be brought in from a nearby well or stream, carried in wooden or leather buckets. The cook peeled and cut up vegetables, herbs and meat on a wooden table.

The Tudors roasted, boiled or baked their food. The children knew that some Tudor cooks roasted meat on long metal rods, called spits, over the fire but they could find no sign of a spit in Pendean. They did find a large pot, called a cauldron, in which meat, vegetables and fruit were boiled.

The cauldron was hung over the hearth on a gadget called a pot crane. Some Tudor chimneys had special openings where fish or meat could be hung to smoke.

The children found they could control the temperature in the cauldron at Pendean with the pot crane and ratchet. They used the pot crane to swing the cauldron over the hottest part of the fire or move it away to the edge of the fire where it could simmer gently. They worked the ratchet to raise the pot from the flames or lower it closer to the fire.

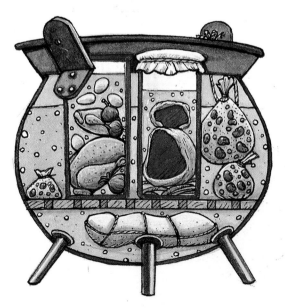

The children read some Tudor recipes. They were surprised that some ingredients had to be caught first. Tudor people trapped rabbits, game birds and water fowl. They used nets and rods to fish, and they caught eels in traps. The children were shocked to find that Tudor people ate herons, cranes, blackbirds, rooks and even beavers.

Most people in Tudor times ate their meals off wooden plates and kept their pewter plates for best. They used knives, and spoons made of horn or pewter, but not forks. Most people, including children, drank ale with their meals. They poured their ale from pottery jugs, or from leather jugs called blackjacks.

Keeping warm

How is your house heated? Do you have central heating that comes on automatically? Perhaps you have real fires which burn logs or coal. In Tudor times everybody heated their houses with fires. The Tudors were the first people since the Romans to produce bricks in large numbers. They used bricks to build fireplaces and chimneys in their houses. Fancy brick chimneys were a sign that the owner of the house was wealthy.

Pendean had a huge fireplace built of brick. The log fire heated about half the house. The children watched how fast the logs burned. When they learned that the fire was kept going all the time, they realised that the Tudors had to gather a lot of fuel.

The children stood well back while the woodcutter chopped the logs. The woodcutter told them that in places where there was no woodland, Tudor people burned heather, gorse or peat. Poor people everywhere burned dried cow dung. The children thought that this must have smelt horrible!

The Tudors stacked wood in a pyramid-shaped pile to keep it dry.

The children wondered why the logs in the hearth were raised on metal stands. They guessed that the stands, which were called fire dogs, allowed air to circulate round the logs. A good fire needs plenty of oxygen to keep it going, so the fire dogs helped the wood burn well. The children found a large metal fork near the fire which they decided must have been used to shift the logs around.

▲

The children found out how to use a tinderbox, which is what people used to light fires before the invention of matches. A worker at the museum struck the flint with a piece of steel to make a spark. The spark was meant to light a little pile of dry straw kept in the tinderbox. But he could not make a spark big enough to light the straw.

21

Keeping clean

In Tudor times people did not know about germs. They did not realise how important it was to wash every day, to do the laundry, and to keep the house clean.

Few Tudor houses had lavatories. Most people went to the lavatory in the fields, made do with buckets, or used chamber pots under the bed. They didn't have toilet paper. They probably used their hands instead. But Bayleaf does have a lavatory, called a garberobe, which is a plank with a hole in it. Although many garderobes emptied into rivers and streams, this one emptied straight into a pit outside.

When the children learned how long it took to wash in Tudor times, they weren't surprised that most people in those days did not wash very often. First they had to fetch the water from the well. They then had to heat it over the fire. They even had to make their own soap from wood ash, quicklime, animal fat and water.

These girls investigated the well. They raised and lowered a bucket on the pulley. The buckets, which were made of wood or leather, were very heavy when full of water. People in Tudor times carried the buckets by hanging them from ropes on a wooden yoke which fitted across their shoulders. This girl tried wearing a yoke with metal chains hanging from it. ►

Housewives washed their bedlinen and clothing only once or twice a year. They washed sheets and blankets, which were heavy when wet, by putting them into the nearest stream and trampling on them. They wrung out the laundry by hand, twisting it to squeeze out the water, and smoothed it with large stones or wooden bats. They dried the laundry flat by hanging it over hedges or pegging it to the ground.

A farmer's wife did not clean out her house very often. She covered the floors with rushes. From time to time she swept the rushes out and replaced them with fresh ones.

Bowls for washing were made of strips of wood, called staves, held together with iron bands. Wooden barrels are still made in this way.

Spinning, weaving and sewing

Tudor women made all their own cloth for clothes, curtains and bedcovers. All women, from the poorest to the richest, spent their spare time spinning, weaving and sewing. Most women left a good supply of household linen in their wills.

Many Tudor households had spinning wheels, and looms for weaving wool and linen thread into cloth. There was no sign of a loom at Bayleaf, but the children did find a spinning wheel which was similar to wheels used in Tudor times. They were surprised how large it was. They found that spinning neat, even thread was much harder than it looked.

Most cloth was made of linen or wool. Linen came from flax plants. The stems were beaten on stones to make linen threads which were woven into cloth for sheets and clothes. Another plant, called hemp, was grown for making rope and a very tough cloth, called canvas.

The children watched a shepherd shear a sheep. The shepherd told them that Tudor wool was much poorer quality than wool today.

Farmers' wives kept some of the wool sheared from the farm sheep to make their own woollen cloth. Poor people gathered wool from hedgerows, where the sheep had rubbed themselves on the brambles.

The children investigated the wool. The spinner told them that before the wool could be spun it had to be washed, and combed or 'carded' so that all the threads ran the same way.

The Tudors dyed their wool and linen with plants and vegetables. The children discovered that wool boiled with onion skins turned a strong orangey-yellow, while wool boiled with nettles turned green.

Embroidery was very popular. Tudor women decorated everything they made using coloured woollen or linen thread. Designs based on flowers, animals and Bible stories were popular. The children thought that sewing must have been difficult without electric lights.

Fun and games

There were no televisions or computer games in Tudor times. People made their own entertainment. In the country, people played music on homemade instruments and sang folk songs. Songs called rounds, where people sing the same tune but join in at different times, were very popular.

There were several important festivals when the whole village would join in the fun. One of the most important was the first day of May when everyone celebrated the coming of spring. People danced round the maypole and played noisy games.

The other great festival was harvest time, when everyone feasted and danced, then went to church services to give thanks for a good harvest.

People in Tudor times enjoyed dancing. This picture shows men and women dancing in a circle to the beat of a drum.

Some cruel sports were popular in Tudor times. Each farmer kept at least one cockerel in the farmyard for cock fighting. People also enjoyed watching bears, bulls and wild pigs, being teased and snapped at by dogs.

This picture shows a variety of activities which Tudor people enjoyed such as skittles and spinning a top. How many other activities can you recognise?

The children were pleased to learn that football was just as popular in Tudor times as it is today. The football was a pig's bladder filled with air. There were lots of people on each side and the goal posts were often in different villages!

The children learnt about a chasing game called 'foxes and chickens' which was popular in Tudor times. They tried playing it themselves outside the barn.

Going to bed

In Tudor times many farmhouses had upstairs rooms. They were used as bedrooms or for storage. In some houses the beds were downstairs. They were sometimes used as comfortable seats for visitors.

This girl climbed the stairs in Pendean. She found them very steep, almost like a ladder.

The children explored the upstairs bedroom in Bayleaf. There they found the big bed where the farmer and his wife slept. Beds similar to this were called 'best beds'. They sometimes had curtains round them. The children also found a truckle bed. All the farmer's younger children slept in it. They also discovered a baby's cradle. They learned that the farmworkers probably slept on coarse straw mattresses downstairs, next to the fire.

The children examined the bedding. They found a thin mattress made of plaited straw on the big bed. Over this was a thick, soft mattress called a flockbed. The flockbed and the pillows were filled with wool, called flock, which wasn't good enough quality to be spun into thread. The blankets were made of wool and the sheets were made of linen.

In Tudor times, wax candles were very expensive. Most people used rushlights to light their houses when it got dark. You can find out how to make a rushlight on page 31. The children lit a rushlight. They found it gave a very dim light and lasted only 20 minutes. They thought that if there was no other light, the house would be quite scary at night.

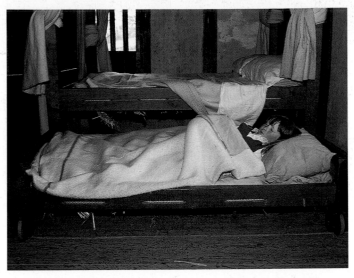

The girl tried the bed. She found the wool-filled mattress was more comfortable than it looked. But she thought the sheets were rough. The truckle bed had small wheels on it. The children guessed that the wheels made it easier to slide the truckle bed under the big bed, where it was kept during the day.

How to find out more

Visits

You can find out much more about living in the country in Tudor times by visiting The Weald and Downland Open Air Museum, Singleton near Chichester, West Sussex, PO18 0EU. Tel: 01243 811 348.

There are many other excellent places you can visit to learn more about life in Tudor times. Among the best are:
The Museum of London, London Wall, London EC2Y 5HN. Tel: 020 7600 3699. This has some of the best displays about Tudor life.

The *Mary Rose* Ship Hall and Exhibition, HM Naval Base Portsmouth PO1 3LR. Tel: 023 9275 0521. This dock contains the remains of the Tudor ship *Mary Rose,* which have been raised from the seabed.

Hampton Court Palace, East Mosely, Surrey, KT8 9AU. Tel: 020 8781 9500. This magnificent palace shows how royalty lived in Tudor times.

For information on Tudor buildings to visit in your area contact:
English Heritage Education Service
Tel: 020 7973 3000;
Historic Scotland
Tel: 0131 668 8600;
The National Trust
Tel: 020 7222 9251.

Things to do

Here are some ideas for things to do which could help you to find out more about life in Tudor times.

Make your own honeysuckle syrup
Most Tudor people living in the country made their own medicines and cures. Try this cure for a sore throat.

You will need: 2½ cups of fresh honeysuckle petals, 300ml of water, 100g sugar, a basin, a wooden spoon, a sieve, a saucepan.

Put 2½ cups of fresh honeysuckle petals into a basin. Crush the petals slightly with a wooden spoon. Pour 300ml of boiling water over them and leave to cool.

Strain the honeysuckle liquid through a sieve into a saucepan and throw the petals away.

Add 100g of sugar and bring slowly to the boil. Simmer until the mixture is syrupy then allow to cool. Pour the syrup into a bottle and seal it. Keep the syrup in a fridge and use it within a week.

Ask an adult to help you with the boiling water.

Bake-ovens for cooking bread and pastries were built into chimneys.

Build your own bake-oven
You will need: about 32 bricks, 3 metal baking trays, wet clay, lots of dry twigs, matches and 'bake your own' bread rolls.

Make a flat base with 10 of the bricks. Build walls two bricks high round three sides.

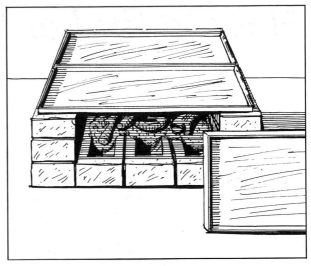

Place two baking trays side by side to form the roof of the oven. Place 10 bricks on top of the trays. Use the third baking tray as the door of the oven.

Light a fire inside the oven using small, dry twigs. Keep the fire going for about half an hour. When the fire has died down, open the door and rake out the ashes.

Put in the bread rolls and seal the door with clay. You could try cooking other things such as bread or biscuits.

Ask an adult to help with this experiment.

Most Tudor people lit their houses with rushlights. How well did they work? Try this experiment and find out.

Rushlights
You will need: some green rushes (these are best cut in the autumn; if you can't find rushes try straw or twisted cotton rags), pieces of animal fat (you can get this from a butcher; sheep fat is best because it dries the hardest), a saucepan, a long narrow tin or dish for dipping the rushes, tweezers, a bulldog clip and a milk bottle.

Cut both ends off a fresh rush, leaving about 20cm. Using tweezers or your fingers, peel the green skin off the rush leaving only a thin strip about 1mm wide along the length of the rush which will hold the pith together.

Melt the fat gently in a saucepan. Pour the melted fat into a long narrow tin. Using the tweezers hold a peeled rush in the fat for about 30 seconds. Take the rush out. Allow to cool and the fat to harden.

Repeat this until you have as many rushlights as you need. Clip a rushlight in a bulldog clip and balance it in a milk bottle. Light one end of the rushlight. How long does the rushlight last?

Ask an adult to help you with melting fat and matches.

Index

First paperback edition 2001

First published 1996 in hardback by
A & C Black (Publishers) Limited
37 Soho Square
London W1D 3QZ

ISBN 0-7136-6280-8

© 1994 A & C Black (Publishers) Limited

A CIP catalogue record for this book is
available from the British Library

This book is dedicated to Chris Zeuner.

Acknowledgements
The authors and publishers would like to
thank the staff of the Weald and Downland
Open Air Museum; West Dean Church of
England School; Sheila Snow; Dave Gabbitas;
Gemma Holder, Paul Holder, Jamie Bevis,
Anna Merriman, Nicolas Smith, Lisa Vivash,
Damian Snow.
All photographs by Maggie Murray except:
p5 (top) County Archivist, West Sussex
Record Office; pp4, 10 (bottom), 11, 24/25
(middle) Richard Palethorpe; pp9 (top), 17
(right), Bob Powell; p23 (bottom) by
permission of the British Library; pp26, 27
(top) The Fotomas Index.

Filmset by Rowland Phototypesetting Ltd,
Bury St Edmunds.
Printed in Italy by LEGO, Vicenza.